Dear Parent:

Reading this story aloud will illustrate the value of sharing. However, it will take a good deal of time, persuasion, and firsthand experience for your young child to become thoroughly convinced.

Don't be discouraged, though. Remember: There isn't an inborn, human inclination to share. On the contrary, "You can't have it—it's mine!" comes naturally to every young child. But there are a number of things that can gradually help alter that. Exhortation from adults is useful, although often it seems to bounce right off those young minds. Small children will acknowledge a belief in sharing if the other person is the sharer—but not when it's the other way around. One typical three-year-old child, when asked to share a toy with his brother, reluctantly handed it over, but then immediately demanded that his sibling share!

But as time goes on and social connections, peer play, and friendship become more valuable, sharing is increasingly seen as a necessity. Like Mr. Bleakman, children learn that if they don't share in all sorts of ways, they can be left friendless. So while it's essential for parents to talk and set the example, it is ultimately the rewards of companionship and friendship that will do the real convincing. So *share* your values generously, but wait patiently for your child's pragmatic self-discovery.

Adele M. Brodkin, Ph.D.

Visit Clifford at scholastic.com/clifford

ISBN 0-439-22463-2

Library of Congress Cataloging-in-Publication Data is available

10 9 8 7 6 5 4 3 2 1   01 02 03 04 05 06

Printed in the U.S.A.   24
First printing, April 2001

Scholastic

Clifford THE BIG RED DOG®

No Dogs Allowed

Adapted by Josephine Page

Illustrated by the Marderosian Studio

**Based on the Scholastic book series
"Clifford The Big Red Dog"
by Norman Bridwell**

From the television script
"The Dog Park" by Pamela Hickey
and Dennys McCoy

Cartwheel
·B·O·O·K·S·®

SCHOLASTIC INC.

New York   Toronto   London   Auckland   Sydney   Mexico City
New Delhi   Hong Kong

Mr. Bleakman was happy

As happy could be

As he sat in the park

On a bench by a tree.

The flowers were blooming.

The birds were in flight.

But the best thing of all—

No dogs were in sight.

He did not like dogs.

And he never could hide it.

He did not like dogs.

And he never denied it.

Mr. Bleakman was happy

As happy could be

As he sat in the park

When whom should he see

But the biggest red dog.

He was shaking the tree!

Said Bleakman, "Stop making

These leaves rain on me!"

He didn't like dogs.

He never could hide it.

He didn't like Clifford

And never denied it.

Mr. Bleakman was angry.

Bleakman was mad.

But Clifford felt sorry.

Clifford was sad.

That's when Clifford gave Bleakman

A lick on the cheek

To make him feel better,

But Bleakman felt wetter

And madder than ever.

He said to the red dog,

"Your lick makes me sick!

Shoo! Go away!

You are ruining my day!"

Mr. Bleakman was happy

As happy could be

When a rare island budgie

Flew into the tree.

Such a marvelous bird!

So pretty and rare!

He tried to get closer,

As close as he'd dare.

Mr. Bleakman loved birds.

He could watch them all day.

He prayed that this birdie

Would not fly away.

Mr. Bleakman was happy

As happy could be

When who should come running

Right under the tree?

Not one dog! Not two dogs!

No, not even three!

But four pesky dogs,

Making noises galore.

They were playing a game

Of four-dog tug-of-war.

Barking and growling,

As doggies will do,

They startled the budgie,

And off that bird flew!

Bleakman didn't like dogs.

He never could hide it.

He didn't like dogs.

He never denied it.

He said, "That's enough!

It's time to get tough!"

Out from the grass,

He pulled up a sign.

He wiped off the dirt.

He pulled off the vine.

He hollered and yelled.

He attracted a crowd.

And read them the sign.

It said, NO DOGS ALLOWED!

The people forgot
What they all knew was true.
No dogs were allowed.
So what could they do?

The sun was still shining.
It wasn't yet dark,
But the dogs and their friends
Were leaving the park.

The very next day,

They all stayed away.

Mr. Bleakman was happy

As happy could be

As he sat in the park

On a bench by a tree.

It was peaceful and quiet.

There wasn't a sound—

Not a dog, not a child,

Not a grown-up around.

So peaceful and quiet,

With no one in sight,

Bleakman said, "This is boring!

This couldn't be right!"

He looked at the sign

And said, "That's the last straw!

No dogs are allowed?

We must change the law!"

So he called an election.

That's what he did.

And everyone voted—

Each grown-up and kid.

The votes were all in.

Bleakman spoke to the crowd.

He said to his neighbors,

"Now dogs ARE allowed!

So come one and all!

Please come! Yes, you may!

Come to the park!

You must come right away

To play with your friends,

To laugh and to bark,

To run and have fun.

It's *everyone's* park!"

Mr. Bleakman is happy
As happy can be
As he sits in the park
On a bench by a tree.

The flowers are blooming.
The birds are in flight.
And grown-ups and children
And dogs are in sight!

Mr. Bleakman likes dogs,

Now that he's tried it.

Bleakman likes dogs.

He never can hide it!

BOOKS IN THIS SERIES:

Welcome to Birdwell Island: Everyone on Birdwell Island thinks that Clifford is just too big! But when there's an emergency, Clifford The Big Red Dog teaches everyone to have respect—even for those who are different.

A Puppy to Love: Emily Elizabeth's birthday wish comes true: She gets a puppy to love! And with her love and kindness, Clifford The Small Red Puppy becomes Clifford The Big Red Dog!

The Big Sleep Over: Clifford has to spend his first night without Emily Elizabeth. When he has trouble falling asleep, his Birdwell Island friends work together to make sure that he—and everyone else—gets a good night's sleep.

No Dogs Allowed: No dogs in Birdwell Island Park? That's what Mr. Bleakman says—before he realizes that sharing the park with dogs is much more fun.

An Itchy Day: Clifford has an itchy patch! He's afraid to go to the vet, so he tries to hide his scratching from Emily Elizabeth. But Clifford soon realizes that it's better to be truthful and trust the person he loves most—Emily Elizabeth.

The Doggy Detectives: Oh, no! Emily Elizabeth is accused of stealing Jetta's gold medal—and then her shiny mirror! But her dear Clifford never doubts her innocence and, with his fellow doggy detectives, finds the real thief.

Follow the Leader: While playing follow-the-leader with Clifford and T-Bone, Cleo learns that playing fair is the best way to play!

The Big Red Mess: Clifford tries to stay clean for the Dog of the Year contest, but he ends up becoming a big red mess! However, when Clifford helps the judge reach the shore safely, he finds that he doesn't need to stay clean to be the Dog of the Year.

The Big Surprise: Poor Clifford. It's his birthday, but none of his friends will play with him. Maybe it's because they're all busy. . . planning his surprise party!

The Wild Ice Cream Machine: Charley and Emily Elizabeth decide to work the ice cream machine themselves. Things go smoothly. . . until the lever gets stuck and they find themselves knee-deep in ice cream!

Dogs and Cats: Can dogs and cats be friends? Clifford, T-Bone, and Cleo don't think so. But they have a change of heart after they help two lost kittens find their mother.

The Magic Ball: Emily Elizabeth trusts Clifford to deliver a package to the post office, but he opens it and breaks the gift inside. Clifford tries to hide his blunder, but Emily Elizabeth appreciates honesty and understands that accidents happen.